*"All this time I've been restraining
myself because I thought you were a
respectable lady. All this time when
you only wanted* this.*"*

He swooped in then and devoured her mouth, ravishing her softness, making no allowance for her smaller size, her femininity. She moaned, whether in pain or desire, she could not tell.

"You should have told me that this is what you wanted." He raised his head to gasp. "I would've obliged you."

She seemed incapable of coherent thought, let alone speech.

"You only had to say the word and I could have taken you on my desk in the library, in the carriage with John Coachman up front, or even here in the garden. God knows I could have tumbled you at any time. Or can't you admit that you want to bed a man whose face looks like mine?"

She tried to shake her head, but it fell helplessly. His hand dropped to her hips and jerked them into his own.

"This is what you crave. What you traveled all the way to London for," he whispered against her mouth.

Advance Praise for *The Raven Prince*

"A sensational debut! Elizabeth Hoyt writes with flair, sophistication, and unstoppable passion . . . will leave you breathless."
—Julianne MacLean, author of *Portrait of a Lover*

"A lively writing style, sparkling dialogue, and lovely, multi-faceted characters."
—Jane Feather, *New York Times* bestselling author